Sunnybrook

a true story with lies...

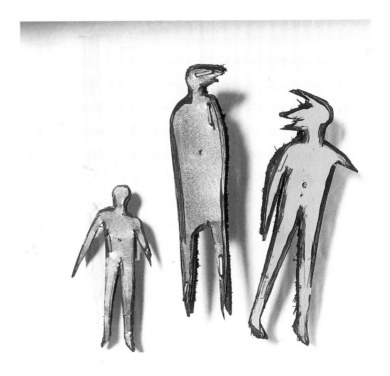

PERSIMMON BLACKBRIDGE

Press Gang Publishers
Vancouver

The Publisher acknowledges financial assistance from the Canada Council, the Book Publishing Industry Development Program of the Department of Canadian Heritage and the Cultural Services Branch, Province of British Columbia.

CANADIAN CATALOGUING IN PUBLICATION DATA
Blackbridge, Persimmon, 1951–
  Sunnybrook

  ISBN 0-88974-068-2 (bound) — ISBN 0-88974-060-7 (pbk.)

  I. Title.
PS8553.L3187S96 1996   C813'.54   C96-910549-5
PR9199.3.B462S96 1996

Jacket and text design by Val Speidel
Cover and text illustrations are details from sculptures by Persimmon Blackbridge, photographed by Susan Stewart © 1996
Black-and-white photographs incorporated into the sculptures are by Chick Rice (p. 4) and Susan Stewart/Kiss & Tell (pp. 35, 48 and 57). The "paintings" in Diane's apartment are by Sally Michener (pp. 9 and 21), Shani Mootoo (p. 11), Deb Bryant (p. 36), Jo Cook (p. 68), and Susan Stewart/Kiss & Tell (pp. 52 and 53). Paintings in Dr. Carlson's office are by Vincent Van Gogh (pp. 4 and 26).
Edited by Barbara Kuhne
Typeset in Fournier and Trixie
Printed by Friesens
Printed on acid-free paper ∞
Printed and bound in Canada

Press Gang Publishers
#101 - 225 East 17th Avenue
Vancouver, B.C. V5V 1A6 Canada
Tel: 604 876-7787   Fax: 604 876-7892

This book is dedicated to

Mary, Stuart, Janey,

Pat, Geneva

and Shirley

ACKNOWLEDGEMENTS

Sunnybrook had an incarnation as an art show before it became a book. Turning it into a book was a peculiar process and I have many people to thank. First is Press Gang Publisher's editor, Barbara Kuhne, who scrawled questions and suggestions all over my tiny manuscript and calmly and confidently told me to come back when it was twice as long. Lizard Jones (a.k.a. my writing group) picked me up off the floor and helped me figure out how to do that. Lorna Boschman held my hand and shared her large experience in transforming one medium into another. Della McCreary held my hand and gave me feedback on every draft of every sentence, supporting and clarifying my new directions with her own experience as a person with learning disabilities. In her role as Press Gang's financial and marketing manager, Della was also responsible for making sure this book could be produced and go out into the world. Susan Stewart photographed all the sculptures in the show (which are now the images in the book), backing her feel for the artwork with years (and years) of technical experience. Irit Shimrat read the new bits with an editor's eye and gave me her mental hospital story for Shirley-Butch. My father, Jack Mitten, named what was missing in my perspective on institutional life and filled it in from his own history as a psychiatric inmate. My mother, Jean Mitten, listened and empathized with every up and down in the process. Sally Michener, my former teacher who has continued over the years to be my mentor, was gently unmerciful in challenging me to go beyond what I knew in both the sculpture and the text. Cynthia Flood, Marc Diamond, Sheila Gilhooly, Monica Chapelle and Ellen Frank gave me invaluable feedback at various stages of the manuscript and reassured me I wasn't (too) crazy. And finally, thank you thank you thank you to designer Val Speidel for her beautiful and wildly inventive work in translating my sculptures and quirky manuscript into a book that is more than a document of an art show.

Sunnybrook

RED CARPET

The Red Carpet Cafeteria was overworked and under-
staffed, the kind of place you work when you can't find
anything else.

    I told them I'd waitressed in a small town in Ontario.

    They didn't check my references.

    The reason I lasted a whole month at the Red Carpet
was because of Surjit, the other countergirl. She told me
what to do, when and how, over and over, day after day.
She said she didn't mind 'cause at least I was a hard
worker, not like the last girl.

    Surjit was always telling me I should get a better job.

    "You have your high school diploma, you could work
in a hospital," she'd say.

    I could see what she meant, of course. The Red Carpet
was run on a very strict system which had to do with
diplomas and also race and sex and age. The dishwashers
were all young South Asian women who didn't speak
English. The cooks were young East Asian men who did.
The cashiers were Anglo women over fifty, and the
manager was a white man. Then there was Surjit and me
on the counter. I knew what she meant about a better job.
I spoke English, I was young and white and diplomaed.

    It turned out Surjit was right, because after a month I
got a call for a job interview at the Sunnybrook Institution
for the Mentally Handicapped.

And I tried.
I had applications
out all over town
and not a single
call.

But I didn't say
they fired me
after one day.

On the other hand,
Surjit was the one
who had the
counter organized
and running like a
beautiful machine,
and I was the one
who dropped a
whole tray of
glasses on the
salad bar. I was
the one who
couldn't even
remember when it
was time for my
break. I was the
one who needed
Surjit's help
to do my job.

THE INTERVIEW

I got the interview at Sunnybrook because I put on my application that I had worked at a child guidance clinic in Ontario.

I went there dressed for success: new panty hose, borrowed shoes, a dress with nice long sleeves that covered the scars on my arms. I was interviewed by Dr. Carlson, the head psychiatrist. I think he wanted to hire someone quickly and get back to his important work. The interview was short.

Actually, I'd been a patient there, but I knew the jargon and I knew the routines, so what the hell.

"So. You're Diane Anderson," he said, checking my application.

"Yes," I said.

"I understand you've worked with teenagers with learning disabilities."

"Yes," I said.

"So you must be used to dealing with some pretty antisocial behaviour."

"Yes," I said.

The word retarded bit like a playground insult in his proper mouth. But that's not the kind of thing you mention in a job interview.

"But you've never worked with retarded people. That's unfortunate. But you do know behaviour mod?"

"Oh yes," I said.

"Good. Very good. Well then. I feel I must tell you: the girl we hired last month for this position quit. One of the residents bit her. Quite badly."

He looked at me. I didn't flinch, and the job was mine.

I know behaviour mod.

FILES

The system at Sunnybrook was simple. You were either nursing staff or psych staff, or an inmate.

The bosses of nursing staff were the nurses. They wore white uniforms. Their underlings were the orderlies. They wore green. The bosses of psych staff were the shrinks, followed by the psychologists and social workers, and then various counsellors like me. We wore regular clothes.

The inmates wore regular clothes too, which was kind of confusing.

My official title was one-to-one counsellor. It was a new concept. It started because the provincial government wanted to take control of the money in this one fund at Sunnybrook. But Sunnybrook didn't want the government to control it. Even though it had just been sitting there for years, they wanted to be the ones who decided how it was spent. So Sunnybrook was fighting with the government about it and at the same time they were spending the money as fast as they could, so that however it was spent they would be the ones who spent it, and how they were spending it was on one-to-one counsellors. My job would last until the money ran out or the government grabbed it, whichever came first.

The pay was five bucks an hour which for me, in 1975, was good money, more than I'd ever made before. I had three people I was working with—"kids," Dr. Carlson called them, even though two of them were older than me.

"You'll understand once you've worked here a while," he said. "They are like kids."

He gave me their files to read. I'd never read anyone's file before, except for my own, when my shrink left the room. It was strange.

I was a professional.

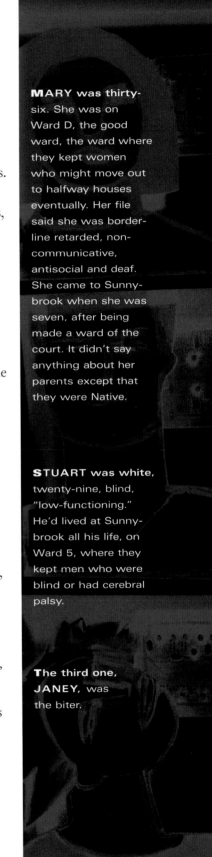

MARY was thirty-six. She was on Ward D, the good ward, the ward where they kept women who might move out to halfway houses eventually. Her file said she was borderline retarded, non-communicative, antisocial and deaf. She came to Sunnybrook when she was seven, after being made a ward of the court. It didn't say anything about her parents except that they were Native.

STUART was white, twenty-nine, blind, "low-functioning." He'd lived at Sunnybrook all his life, on Ward 5, where they kept men who were blind or had cerebral palsy.

The third one, **JANEY,** was the biter.

TRUTH

Sunnybrook sprawled out with green lawns and seven or eight big buildings. Like a college campus except for the wire mesh over the windows, and the fence. I had keys. A key for the main gate, keys for the staffrooms, keys for Ward 5, Ward D and the bad ward, Ward B.

I was scared, my first day at work. I wasn't scared of the nurses and orderlies and psych staff. They were busy. They ignored me. I was scared of the other people, the "residents" as we were supposed to call them. They were weird. I'd never seen so many weird-looking people in my life. At the child guidance clinic we were all normal-looking unhappy kids and teenagers. But this was different. This was hundreds of people and you could tell just by looking at them that they didn't belong to the free world. Someone had locked them up. They were locked-up people.

I spent the first few days walking around clutching my keys. But it changed. People got names. Faces got familiar. They lived on Ward D or said good morning to me or laughed when my socks didn't match.

I remember one day after I'd been there a few weeks. I was hanging out with Stuart, sitting on a bench, petting

the grass, when some floats from the Canada Day Parade drove through the grounds. Probably they did it every year as an act of charity; I don't know.

I remember when the float with Miss Salmon Queen and her court drove by. I could see the shock freezing her perfect smile as she waved at Stuart with his Frankenstein face.

I wanted to throw a rock at her.

STUART

Stuart was about six foot four and really did look a lot like Frankenstein's monster.

He sat in the dayroom on Ward 5 with his face turned toward the noise of the TV, and rocked back and forth.

Diane had never seen anyone who looked like Stuart, except in the movies as a monster. He was too big to be a poor little poster kid.

There were a lot of people rocking back and forth. One of the orderlies brought me over to Stuart.

"Say 'Hello Diane,' " he said.

"Hello Diane," Stuart said. His voice was soft and hollow. His eyes were blind. I sat down next to him.

"How are you, Stuart?" I asked.

"How are you, Stuart?" he answered, still rocking.

Across the room, another orderly looked up from tying someone's shoes.

"Take him off the ward. He never gets off the ward."

"Want to go outside?" I asked.

My orders from Dr. Carlson were to improve Stuart's language skills, but I could do that off the ward.

Stuart rocked. I took his hand and pulled. He stood up. We walked. I opened the door with my big Ward 5 key. We went outside.

Stuart tasted the air and laughed, a kind of joyous snort. We crossed the lawn slowly, Stuart laughing and holding my hand.

I felt kind of awkward. I wasn't used to holding hands with big huge men.

I tried to remember what Anne Bancroft did with Patty Duke in *The Miracle Worker*. I walked him over to a tree and put his hand on it.

"Tree," I said.

"Tree," he repeated.

He explored the tree, touching it carefully with fingertips, palms and face, breathing its smell, frowning in concentration. I said "Tree." He said "Tree."

That seemed good.

We did a lamppost, grass, sidewalk, bushes. He liked the bushes best. He opened his arms and walked into the thick hedge, laughing.

"Bushes," I said.

"Bushes," he said.

When our hour was up, I took him back to Ward 5 and left him, rocking, his face turned toward the noise of the TV.

TYPING

Every week, I had to write a report on the progress my "clients" were making. The first one I did, Dr. Carlson gave back to me. He said they had to be typed. I felt stupid. I mean, it was written in ink; I thought that would be good enough. I had a lot to learn about being a professional.

Lots of people can't type, but some people really can't type. I belong to the second variety. Writing by hand is kind of problematic too, which is why I like to write in pencil. Pencil you can erase. Ink is harder. Typing is a whole other world, and I don't live in it.

Luckily for me, I'm a lesbian, and I often have girl-friends who can type. I suppose lots of men type too, these days, so even if I was straight I'd still be OK. But that's not something I worry about too much.

9

MARY

I liked Ward D. There were lots of friendly people there—Shirley, Pat, Geneva . . . In fact, everyone there liked me except Mary. Mary liked to sit by herself and look out the window. She didn't like people bugging her. But I had to bug her or I'd get fired for not doing my job.

Dr. Carlson gave me two books on sign language and told me to teach Mary to sign. The first book was a big thick one called *American Sign Language: A Linguistic Analysis*. The second was a skinny book with lots of pictures of what the signs were for different words. I figured I'd start with the pictures and work my way up. I had a few days to study my book; then I went to meet Mary.

Nurse Thompson, the head nurse on Ward D, took me over to where Mary was staring out the window. Mary glared at her for a second, and then looked away.

"You do know behaviour mod?" Nurse Thompson asked.

"Oh, yes," I said.

"Well behaviour mod is a little tricky with kids like Mary. And not just because she can't speak or hear. The form of negative conditioning we like at Sunnybrook is withdrawing attention."

"Of course," I said.

"On Ward B, that means a few hours in the sideroom, which is your basic solitary confinement."

"Right."

"Here on Ward D, we put them on a chair in the hallway and everyone ignores them for a while. It's humane, it's effective. Except with kids like Mary who are so antisocial they would just as soon be ignored."

It didn't matter that no one else on Ward D knew how to sign. It didn't matter that Diane didn't know how to sign. She could learn from the books and teach Mary. Then Mary would have a way to communicate in case anyone who did know sign happened to drop by the ward.

Nurse Thompson laughed and shook her head.

"In cases like Mary's, we use good old positive reinforcement. It's really just as effective."

Nurse Thompson reached in her pocket, pulled out a chocolate bar, and held it in Mary's line of sight. Mary looked up. Nurse Thompson gave me the chocolate bar and pointed to me, then to Mary, then to me again.

"Just show her a candy bar before you start each session, and give it to her at the end. I think you'll find her quite co-operative. She loves chocolate. We never see her eat it though. She always puts it in that little plastic purse she has and eats it later, secretly, when no one is watching. Strange rituals these kids have." She laughed again.

Mary and I worked on signs for the rest of the afternoon. I'd point to things in the room and sign the words for them until she could repeat them.

Other women on the ward kept coming by, introducing themselves and asking questions. It was better than TV. It was new.

But Mary wasn't impressed. She worked with sullen, angry energy. She was amazingly fast. I would have thought that the concept of signs would be a tough one.

Especially for someone like Mary, with below normal intelligence.

At the end of our time, I gave her the candy bar. She put it in her purse, and then she held her hand out to me.

I put my hand in hers.

"Thank you, Mary," I said.

She grabbed hold of one of my fingers and pulled it back, hard. I yelled. It really hurt.

Nurse Thompson looked up from her desk. "Oh, I forgot to tell you. She does that."

I could have said that maybe Mary hated being controlled and wanted to keep what she could of her dignity. I could have said that it was an admirable thing. And Nurse Thompson could have complained about me to Dr. Carlson.

As tough as learning to use words.

She's not that bad, I thought. I'm winning her over already.

NURSE HOLLY

One of the best places in Sunnybrook was the staff washroom in the basement of the administration building. No one ever used it, not even the maintenance staff.

If you had keys, you could go in there and close the door and know that no one would ever come in, or even knock on the door. I used to go down to that washroom for my breaks or even my lunch hour. I would just sit there doing nothing, thinking nothing.

Or maybe I would cry.

The only sign I saw that anyone else ever went there was when I found a book on the back of the toilet. It was called *Honeymoon for Nurse Holly*.

At first I ignored it, but when it was still there after a few days, I started reading it. It was a little bit boring, but also kind of soothing. Like you knew just what was going to happen, and you didn't really care.

*T*he story was about this woman, *Holly*, who graduates from nursing school and comes to work in a **big** hospital. *R i g h t   a w a y* she starts having **trouble** with this handsome but arrogant doctor

...

JANEY

I was at Sunnybrook for a couple of weeks before I started on Ward B. But when I reported in to the Ward B office, Nurse Jones told me Janey was locked in the sideroom.

"She'll be in there for another hour or two. You might as well take a break."

I sat in the staffroom. No one else was there. I didn't feel like reading old magazines or writing my weekly report.

I went back out to the dayroom. It was nothing like the dayroom on Ward D. Ward B had a bare concrete floor and no TV, no pictures on the wall, no curtains over the barred windows.

But there were lots of people and they were all shouting except for the ones who were sitting in corners with their eyes closed. There was an orderly sweeping up broken glass. He nodded to me and kept on working.

I went back down the hall, past door after locked door. One door had a window in it, with bars and safety glass. Inside, I could see a woman in a strait jacket.

I knew it was a strait jacket even though I'd never seen one before.

The room was small and square, with a tiny high window that didn't let in much light. The woman was singing.

It had to be the sideroom and it had to be Janey.

I stood there for a minute and then I unlocked the door. It locked behind me, automatically, like all the doors in Sunnybrook.

When she saw me, Janey started to scream, kind of a high quiet scream through clenched teeth. An anxiety scream.

I could understand that. I was feeling a little anxious too, and I had keys and no strait jacket.

I backed into the corner by the door, and we stood on our opposite sides watching each other. After a while she stopped screaming.

"So, umm, hi Janey," I said.

"Hi Janey," she said.

"My name's Diane," I said.

"My name's Diane," she said.

I knew all about the repeating thing by now. According to Dr. Carlson, it was this bad mental illness called echolalia, and I was supposed to cure people of it.

Janey and I kept on watching each other. Now and then she would scream for a second, but mostly she talked — a different kind of talk, which I'm sure had some big name too.

"Bad girl," she said. "Broke the window. No, no. Don't break the window. Go to the sideroom. Bad girl. Don't break the cup. Don't break the plate. Go to the sideroom. Bad girl."

Every time she said "bad girl" she'd hit the back of her head against the wall. I said "Hi Janey" a couple of times just to change the subject, and she said "Hi Janey" to me. Then she started singing again. It was the title song from *The Sound of Music*. She knew all the words.

"The hills are alive with the sound of music," she sang.

I noticed there was shit smeared on the window. That's why not much light came through. It was dry and dusty, like it had been there for months.

"My heart will be blessed with the sound of music," Janey sang. After a while I sang with her, even though I didn't know the words.

I'd impressed Dr. Carlson with my great behaviour mod plan for Stuart. I said I would ignore him unless his words were appropriate and responsive. I said I learned that method at the child guidance clinic, but it wasn't actually from there. It was from before that. It was how I had learned to talk. However, I didn't intend to use it on Stuart or Janey. It was for Dr. Carlson.

BEHAVIOUR MOD

There were two versions of how I learned to talk. The first was one of those funny family stories that you hear all your life. In that version, my older sister talked so much that I couldn't get a word in edgewise. Finally, when I was three, she was sent off to nursery school and then I learned to talk.

The second version I only heard once. I had just come back from Ontario, and my mother and I were sitting around drinking wine. I was telling her about my adventures as a waitress and disturbed teen, and she was correcting my grammar.

She was awfully big on grammar for someone who was thrown out of half the high schools in her home town.

Then all of a sudden she started crying and saying that sometimes she wondered if she should have raised me differently. I asked her what she meant and this whole story spilled out:

I don't remember what I said. I was a little stunned. But now I put these words in Diane's mouth: You were scared and you hurt me to protect me, as mothers sometimes do. You were afraid that the world would rip me apart. Because you knew the world. You knew it when your mother was taken away and put in a psych ward. You knew it when you were a teenager, expelled from school after school. And I also know the world. We try to pass. We know the consequences.

By the time you were three, you only had a few words. But you had sounds and gestures and a whole elaborate way of communicating. We usually understood you, but if we didn't, your sister would interpret for you. She always knew what you were saying. But you weren't learning to talk. We had to do something. We sent Michelle to nursery school, and I started doing this program with you, at home alone all day. I would ignore you unless you used words. If you told me in your other language that you wanted a glass of water, I would ignore you. Or if you wanted to go outside. Or anything. You were so angry, you would cry and scream and throw yourself on the floor. You didn't understand. There was no way to explain it to you. Finally you gave up and started talking.

So anyhow, that was my great behaviour mod ignoring technique that I used, years later, to impress Dr. Carlson.

SHIRLEY

The first time I met Shirley, she was sitting on a chair in the hallway on Ward D.

"Hi," she said, "who are you?"

"My name's Diane. I work with Mary."

"Oh boy, Mary. Better work with Pat instead." She shook her head. "Mary. Oh boy."

I wondered just what she knew about Mary. Maybe Mary had tried to break her fingers. But somehow, looking at Shirley, I doubted it.

"I just do what they tell me to. And they told me to work with Mary."

I thought maybe I should ask Shirley a few things about Ward D, things I didn't think Nurse Thompson would tell me, but just then an orderly came running up to us yelling "Don't talk to her!"

"Go away," Shirley told her. "We're busy."

"Umm, what's wrong?" I asked.

"You're supposed to ignore them when they're on that chair. It's behaviour mod," the orderly said.

"Oh yeah, right," I said.

"Excuse me," Shirley said, "I'm talking to this lady. She's telling me about her job which is not a very good one."

The orderly smiled at me, turning her back to Shirley. "Don't worry about it. You're new here, you'll learn. But you've got to watch out for Shirley. She's a troublemaker. You'll see. She's a real manipulator. And she talks too much. And another thing: she's a lesbian. So be careful."

"How do you know?" I asked.

"It's in her file."

"Oh," I said. "OK."

I looked at Shirley. She rolled her eyes.

The orderly ignored her.

It was behaviour mod.

I couldn't think of anything else to say.

RUNNING

Janey and I went off the ward
whenever we could. We didn't care if
it was raining or what, we were gone.
We went to the same places and did
the same things, every day. That's
what Janey liked. Having fun was our
main thing.

Doing things that sounded good on
my weekly report to Dr. Carlson was
a secondary consideration.

On the ward we behaved ourselves.
Or at least I behaved myself, getting
Janey's coat on her, making sure she
had the right shoes, while Janey
bounced off the walls, trying to hug me
and talk to me and pull me out the door.

I can't hug you,
Janey.

"How are you, Janey?" I asked.

"How are you, Janey?" she repeated,
pushing her coat away.

"How are YOU, Janey?" I repeated.

"How are YOU, Janey?" she
repeated.

I held her shoulders and looked at her,
hard. "HOW ARE YOU, JANEY?"

"Fine," she said.

"Do you want to go outside?"

Dumb question.
I was full of dumb
questions. But she
was supposed to
learn to hold
still for dumb
questions.

"Outside. Yes."

We walked sedately down the sidewalk, until we were out of sight from the
Ward B windows. Then we ran. That's
what we did, every day. That's what Janey
liked. She was an athlete, despite years of
sitting around on the ward and those
starchy meals. Maybe tension kept her

hard. She vibrated with tension. She was vibrant. Her body couldn't hold it all.

No wonder she bit people and broke windows. No wonder she ran tearing across the lawns, laughing, running in circles around me with breath left for singing at the top of her lungs, jumping for the tall maple trees, bursting into the air with wild shouts and an elegant flick of fingers on one high-flung leaf, running backwards, grinning at me, a dangerous inmate who I could never hope to catch.

Running might take the edge off all that energy and keep Janey out of the sideroom. Maybe, if we were lucky, if nothing heavy happened on the ward, if no one pushed her too hard, too fast. Keeping Janey out of the sideroom was my other main thing.

Going back on the ward was tough. Janey always wanted me to give her my keys so she could unlock the big front door herself. I couldn't risk anyone seeing that. I'd say no, carefully, and poke her in the belly with my keys until she laughed.

Inside, we'd hang around in the hallway, cooling out, and then I'd ease Janey into the dayroom and say good-bye.

Sometimes she'd want to hug me and keep me there as long as she could. Other times she'd just look away, leaning against the wall with her arms folded across her chest, a muscle jumping in her jaw.

I can't hug you, Janey. I know that no one here ever hugs you, and that you've lived here all your life. You were a child in this cold place. I know you're starved for simple affection, but I can't hug you, not here. I have to be careful and keep up appearances, and never let anyone get the wrong idea. These are the rules for queers. Even when I'm invisible, their judgements are inside me, singing through my nerves like fear, binding my arms when you reach for me. That's life, Janey. Life in the free world.

FREE WORLD

One night I was wandering around downtown when
I saw Stuart in a leather jacket, leaning against a building,
smoking a cigarette and looking cool.

A few days later, I saw Mary at McDonald's, eating a
Double Cheeseburger and arguing with this good-looking
guy.

And the next week, I saw Janey, playing softball in the
park. She was the best one on the team.

Then I saw Pat on the bus, laughing and talking in
Cantonese with two other women and five children.

And I saw Shirley at Sappho's, dancing and flirting and
causing a commotion.

I had to walk
right up to him to
before I realized
it wasn't Stuart
at all. It was
just some guy. He
wasn't even tall.

But it wasn't
them. Of course it
wasn't them. They
were locked up.

LESBIAN SOCIAL SERVICE PROFESSIONAL

My girlfriend said if I was having such a hard time at work, maybe I should join the Lesbian Social Service Professionals' Support Group. I could talk about my job to people who would really understand, and avoid Social Service Burnout.

I went to Sappho's instead and downed five Blues in quick succession. Shirley was there, a hallucination, sitting at a table of loud butches. That was OK. At this point in my life, hallucinations didn't worry me too much. I shot sneaky glances at her between beers, and considered my life.

I hadn't actually explained to my girlfriend about the child guidance clinic and the lie on my job application. I hadn't told her about my current official diagnosis, or the one before that. I hadn't really gone into my spotty employment record in any detail. She knew I couldn't type or drive or fill out forms, because she helped me with that kind of thing. She knew about my scars because I did occasionally take my long-sleeved shirts off. I wasn't sure what she thought about it all. I guess she thought I should go to a Lesbian Social Service Professionals' Support Group. It didn't really make sense.

I had another Blue. Then I switched to tequila to see if I could find wisdom there. No luck. Then Shirley sat down beside me.

"Are you trying to pick me up or what?" she said.

No one knew about the child guidance clinic except for my friends in Ontario who were mad at me for being too weird, and my mother, who thought it was funny. Something about the idea of her hulking teenaged daughter sitting in the waiting room amidst the Lego and teddy bears.

ROCK ME

It wasn't actually Shirley. She was taller, with a butch swagger that the real Shirley could have punctured with one pointed remark. Unfortunately I wasn't that sharp.

"I was just—I wasn't—you look like someone I know," I stuttered.

"Oooh, I've heard that one before," Shirley-Butch replied. "Haven't we met? Somehow, somewhere, across a crowded room? Wanna dance?"

"Sure," I said.

We danced. I was a bit unsteady on my feet but so were half the other babes on the dance floor.

Shirley-Butch had a casual, too-cool-to-dance shuffle. She wore these sort of pressed polyester pants and a bowling shirt instead of jeans and tank tops like everyone else. But she was cute. She had big shoulders and crooked teeth. She had the same out-of-control red hair as Shirley. As "Rock Me Baby" segued to "Love to Love You," she pulled me into a slow dance that made my palms sweat.

"I think I have to go," I yelled, barely audible over Donna Summers' disco orgasm.

"And here I thought you were coming home with me tonight." She pushed her pelvis a little tighter into mine and then stepped back.

"I can't. I, umm, have a girlfriend and all."

"You looked more like a girl getting very drunk all by herself than a girl with a girlfriend. But I guess I was wrong."

She blew me a kiss and disappeared back to her table.

It was the least stupid thing I could think of.

Diane would never have used the word babes *in 1975.*

THE LINE

Getting up in the morning was the worst thing. ← Especially if I'd been up late the night before acting like a fool at Sappho's.
The alarm clock grabbed my brain and shook it, like a
Pit Bull with a Pekingese. My first emotion of the day was
startled terror, followed by the slow, ugly realization that
I had to go to work.

My girlfriend had bought me a clock radio while I was
at the Red Carpet. She thought I could slide into
wakefulness on a gentle tide of Chopin or Brahms. But
I never listened to classical stations, so like as not it was
the gentle tide of some Top 40 DJ who probably hated
his job too.

Breakfast was a piece of toast at the bus stop, and a
take-out coffee from my local McDonald's. It was a West
Coast theme McDonald's, featuring frolicking killer
whale wallpaper; hard to take at 8:00 a.m., but coffee
is coffee.

This was back when McDonald's had themes: cowboys in Calgary and surfers in San Diego. Now all the parts are pretty much interchangeable around the world: something to depend on.

I had to take two buses, the local to downtown and then
the suburban express. Like most institutions, Sunnybrook
was stuck out at the raw edge where industry was dying
and people needed the jobs even more than they feared
the inmates. It was a long ride.

I would sit in the back and look at the ads. Sometimes
there was a new one, but usually they were the same from
week to week. You could tell a lot from an ad, like which
companies had the money to hire graphic designers. The
ugliest ad on the bus had this awkward pencil drawing
of a little kid sitting at a school desk with his face all
scrunched up in tears or anger. There was a big caption
over it: "Is your child BRIGHT, but having trouble
LEARNING?" Underneath was the phone number of a
society for parents of children with learning disabilities
that you could call for help. I stared at that ad every day
on the long dull ride to work. The layout was lousy, but
I had no trouble reading the message.

Your child is bright, the ad said. He's nearly normal. He's on the right side of the line, the bloody gash that separates OK-human from pitiful monster. On the wrong side of the line is an entirely different sort of thing, a thing that gets people teased, avoided, stared at, locked up. They have a different name for it, it has to be different. Please make it be different.

SIGNING (SORT OF)

Ward D was fixed up better than some of the other wards, but it wasn't exactly relaxing to work there. There were always four or five people trying to talk to me, and Nurse Thompson watching from her office, and Mary waiting for a chance to break my fingers.

Maybe that's why it took me so long to figure things out.

"Will you teach me how to sign?" Geneva asked. She was leaning over the back of the couch with her pals Pat and Shirley, preferring Mary's battles to the old black-and-white war movie on afternoon TV.

"Sorry, Geneva," I said. "You're not deaf, you don't need to learn to sign."

I signed to Mary to point to the red book. She pointed to the red book.

"Only deaf people can sign?" Geneva asked.

"Well, no—I mean—forget I said that. I can't teach you because they told me to just teach Mary. That's why."

I signed to Mary to point to the blue book. She replied with a fast mess of signs, most of which I couldn't understand. "Wrong," I signed. She glared at me.

"Hey, Diane. Mary doesn't like you," Shirley said.

"I know," I said.

I asked Mary about the blue book again. She pointed to the blue book.

"Mary can hear, you know," said Pat.

"Well she puts on a good act, then."

I pointed to a picture of a car and asked what it was. Mary told me it was a car.

"She can so hear," Shirley said.

Making conversation with Mary was slow going.

24

"Well, kind of," Pat said.

"Oh yeah," I said.

I asked about a picture of a house. Mary answered with another fast series of incomprehensible signs.

"Will you teach me how to sign?" Geneva asked.

I didn't scream. I turned around and said in a loud voice, "If you guys don't quit bugging me, I'll tell Nurse Thompson."

Pat and Geneva backed away quickly. Shirley was more leisurely, sauntering off saying, "OK, nurse. Bye, nurse."

"I'm not a nurse," I yelled after her. ←————— Shirley knew how to get to me.

I asked Mary about the house again. She went slower this time, and I still didn't understand. "Wrong," I signed. "Wrong," she signed back. "Wrong, wrong, wrong."

I thought about it.

I was a little slow, but I was catching on.

25

DR. CARLSON

I had a meeting about Mary, with Dr. Carlson. He sat behind his big desk, making notes in a file.

Mary's file, or mine, I didn't know.

"I think Mary's pretty smart," I said.

"Yes, of course. She's only borderline retarded. Certainly compared to your other clients she's on the bright side."

"No, I mean she's very smart."

Dr. Carlson sighed. "I know, it's confusing at first. Some of these kids can be clever and manipulative. But that's quite different from actual intelligence. You'll understand once you've worked here awhile."

I didn't tell him that Mary was one of the most straightforwardly rude people I'd ever met in my life and she certainly never bothered to manipulate anyone. ←——— *She didn't tell him that many deaf people have been thrown in institutions when hearing people didn't know how to talk to them. She didn't know that in 1975.*

Instead, I nodded in a respectful kind of way and said, "She's picking up signing really fast."

"That's excellent," Dr. Carlson said, making a note in the file.

"In fact," I said, "I wonder if she knew signing before. Before she came here. I think she knows signs I never taught her."

"That's certainly a possibility." Dr. Carlson smiled. "Must make your job a lot easier, eh?" He made another note and closed the file, time-to-go signals in the universal language of shrinks.

I wanted to shake him. I wanted to scream: think about it! Mary knew how to sign as a child. Did her parents teach her? Did she talk with her parents in sign? And then the court took her away, as so many Native children are taken away. And they put her in this place where no one could talk to her. Is that what happened? Did she try to speak in sign, those first long weeks? And did you ignore her?

But I didn't say it. I couldn't. I was making it all up anyway. It wasn't in her file. Instead, I said good-bye politely, and went off to the staff washroom. I wanted to cry, but I couldn't. There were no tears. I picked up *Honeymoon for Nurse Holly*.

Holly was

Dr. Peters because s.

nice enough

but you could tell th

a very   c

under his br

ng a *fight* with

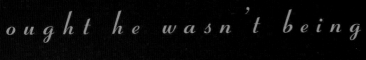

ought he wasn't being

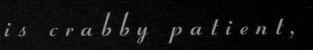

is crabby patient,

Dr. Peters was really

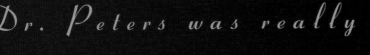

ing person

que exterior.

MARY ISN'T

The reason she called me Persimmon was because it was my other name, the name my friends called me. Only shrinks and landlords and people at work called me Diane.

"Jesus, Persimmon, it makes me so mad!" my girlfriend said, typing furiously on my weekly report. "Mary doesn't belong in that place!"

"None of them do," I said.

"Well yeah, but Stuart and Janey. . . it sounds like they really are seriously brain damaged. You know? And Mary isn't."

They shouldn't be in that place, I thought to myself. After a few minutes, I said it out loud.

"Yeah, but what's the alternative?" my girlfriend asked. "Do you really think they could get along in the outside world?"

I had already considered this problem. It was the main unworkable element that had forced me to abandon my kidnapping scheme. I was silent for a long time and then finally I said, "Things could be different. Like big things. It's possible."

"Yeah," my girlfriend said. "Don't hold your breath."

She could type and talk at the same time. It was impressive.

GREAT IDEA

My next great idea was that I would get Mary to teach me how to sign.

To acknowledge her expertise and put her in a more powerful role would be a good thing, maybe even a breakthrough.

I tried it for the rest of the week. Mary used the opportunity to try to break my fingers.

MONDAY, MONDAY

I took my bruised fingers to Sappho's and soaked them in alcohol. Mary was a bitch, I told myself. I was always friendly to her and tried to intervene with Dr. Carlson on her behalf and I was probably the nicest staff person on Ward D, and she still didn't like me. She didn't like me any more than she liked Nurse Thompson. It wasn't fair.

It was a Monday night, and Sappho's was nearly deserted. There was a couple-in-love holding hands over a little table in the corner, and a grumpy young bull dyke at the other end of the bar. This time I'd skipped the preliminaries and gone straight to tequila.

I kept watching the door as if I was expecting someone. Eventually another couple-in-love showed up, and bopped enthusiastically to "Get Up Off of That Thing" by James Brown.

How could it only be Monday night? How could I get through Tuesday? I kept watching the doorway, but she never showed up.

Not a disco-bunny Sunrise, but straight up in one of those glasses with salt on the rim, like a real tough drinker would have.

In your dreams. This is a regular dyke bar owned by some straight businessman or the Mafia or something and the music all comes out of a can marked "No R&B Need Apply."

31

PLASTIC FLOWER-THINGS

Every time I came to Ward 5, Stuart was sitting on the same chair, in the same corner. Today the TV was tuned to some soap opera.

"Hi Stuart," I said.

He stopped rocking and took my hand, pressing it into his face, breathing my smell.

"Diane," he said. He ran his fingers over my face. He had big, soft hands and this delicate way of touching, kind of fluid, like his fingers had extra joints.

"How're you doing, Stuart?" I asked.

"Outside," he said.

I sat down next to him. "No, we can't go outside yet. Nurse Lau wants me to teach you how to shave."

He started rocking again, just a bit, waiting for whatever was going to happen next. All the other Ward 5 guys were rocking too. Most of them were blind but some had cerebral palsy. Some of them were strapped into their chairs to keep them from sliding onto the floor. None of them tried to talk to me. Ward 5 was a speak-when-you're-spoken-to kind of place. I put the electric shaver that the nurse had given me into Stuart's hands. After he'd felt it, I plugged it in and turned it on.

"Shaving," I said.

"Shaving," he said.

I went through the whole routine: holding the razor, running it over his face, feeling for spots he'd missed.

I'd never seen it before but I knew it was a soap opera because it had soap opera music.

That always embarrassed me.

I hoped I was doing it right. It wasn't like I'd had any practice with it.

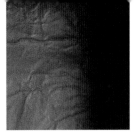

Stuart did OK. He always did OK, as long as someone paid attention to him. But as soon as he was left alone, he'd lapse into rocking.

After shaving, we went outside. Stuart liked to wander around and feel the trees and buildings. He liked the painted-over rust on the perimeter fence, the rough cement benches near Ward 3. And the grass.

He was learning the names for lots of things, but it was just because he was such a friendly and accommodating kind of guy. He wasn't really interested in words.

We walked over to a low building with aluminum siding. There were some good bushes below the barred windows. Stuart explored them, leaf by leaf.

Through the windows, I could see a big room with rows of long tables. There were people sitting at the tables, bent over piles of pink plastic. They were making those round plastic flower-things, like you put on cars at weddings.

I recognized Shirley at one of the tables toward the back. She had a big heap of pink plastic on one side of her, and a big heap of pink plastic flower-things on the other side of her. She didn't see me.

"Let's go, Stuart," I said.

But Stuart was smelling the leaves and laughing.

"Bushes," he said.

I could see how it was a good thing, on Ward 5, to be able to space out like that instead of going totally screaming mad from boredom.

BUSY

The next time I saw Shirley, she was sitting with Geneva on the stone bench across the lawn from Ward D. I was a bit early for my session with Mary, so I sat down next to them.

"Hi guys," I said.

Geneva jumped up. "I have a pass!"

"Yeah, I know, it's fine." As a well-behaved and responsible Ward D resident, Geneva always had grounds privileges. Shirley was another story, but luckily for me, policing Shirley wasn't in my job description.

"So whatcha up to?" I asked.

Geneva shifted from foot to foot. "Your purse strap is broken," she said.

"What do you want?" asked Shirley.

"Nothing, really," I said. "Just thought I'd say hi."

"We're busy," Shirley said. "Go away."

"Oh. OK," I said. At least she didn't call me nurse. I checked my watch, trying to look like a busy professional instead of a social reject.

"Well, see you," I said. Seven more minutes. Nurse Holly here I come.

Spending even a few extra minutes on the ward was not a big priority in my life.

Geneva was always pointing out little flaws in my cover. She had a good eye for normal. She worked hard at it. If she kept it up, she'd get out of this place and into some boarding home where there'd be a fresh set of rules for her to learn. I was rooting for her. Go, Geneva, go.

FRIENDS

I tried to imagine myself talking with Nurse Thompson the way Holly did with her friends, joking and sharing girlish confidences. It didn't seem possible. I was only twenty-two but I was already too old.

There was this young blond intern who seemed to be interested in Holly. He was kind of easy going and good humoured, and all Holly's nurse friends thought she had made a great conquest. But Holly was strangely drawn to that dark-haired, brooding Dr. Peters . . .

COOL

The bartender at Sappho's knew me by this time. She had my tequila in front of me almost before my butt hit the bar stool.

I think they call that codependence, but not in 1975.

Shirley-Butch was dancing with a sleek dyke who I'd seen before at some demo, but not dressed like that. I think she belonged to the Revolutionary Workers' League in her other life, but in this life she wore a red dress that paid homage to her cleavage and the most exquisitely funky platform shoes ever seen on a non-drag queen. Unfortunately, she couldn't quite dance in them.

They hung in through "Shining Star" and "Way of the World" by Earth, Wind and Fire, looking pretty cozy, but Shirley-Butch dumped her, cleavage and all, at the end of "YMCA" and went back to sit with her loud friends.

Either she didn't try to pick up every chick she danced with, or it was too early in the night to make her move, or she wasn't turned on by platform shoes.

Two tequilas later, I cruised over to Shirley-Butch's table and asked her to dance. I could see her friends looking at each other out of the corners of their eyes and stifling smiles.

Shirley-Butch leaned back in her chair and looked me up and down. "My, my, it's the girl with the girlfriend," she said. "Will wonders never cease?"

The dance floor was crowded with sweaty flesh on flesh, hot lights strobing through my brain, bass-line to my heart. Shirley-Butch danced cool and slow and didn't ask me home.

Either she had told them she liked me, or she had told them she didn't like me, or my outfit was all wrong.

BURN DOWN

The next time I saw Shirley, she was sitting in the day-room on Ward B, the bad ward, wearing a green bathrobe and fuzzy slippers. I'd never seen anyone at Sunnybrook in a bathrobe before.

Proper dress was strictly enforced as a sign of normality.

I'd also never seen anyone hanging out on a ward where they didn't live. Sunnybrook wasn't exactly a visiting back and forth kind of place, and Shirley was a Ward D person.

"Hey nurse, what are you doing here?" Shirley said.

"I'm not a nurse," I said. "What are you doing here?"

Shirley grinned. "I made a fire," she said.

"Oh," I said. I thought for a minute. "What for?" I asked.

"To burn down Sunnybrook," she said.

I squashed my impulse to say "right on."

"Oh," I said. "So, umm, what happened?"

"I burned up Nurse Thompson's waste basket. There was smoke and fire alarms but then it went out. Now I have to stay on Ward B for awhile. They're mad." Shirley smirked.

"Oh," I said. "Wow."

"It wasn't a very good fire," Shirley said. "Do you know much about fires?"

It was a bit lame, but I didn't know what else to say. Shirley often had that effect on me.

This conversation was taking a distinctly awkward turn. I didn't think encouraging this sort of thing was in my job description. "You know, Shirley," I said cautiously, "people can get really hurt in fires."

"Well excuse me, nurse! I'll be more careful next time."

"My name is Diane," I said.

"Yeah, right," she said.

I went off to the sideroom to find Janey.

SKIN

Janey, your

arms are

scar on scar.

Toothmarks

track you

layer on layer

year on year.

I've seen you

tear your

skin to blood

and skin

is strong.

How can

someone

bite

that hard?

I guess

you use what

you can get.

I use a

razor.

NUTHOUSE

"You work in a nuthouse?" Shirley-Butch sat up, holding onto her tangled hair as if her head was about to fall off. "I can't believe I'm in bed with someone who actually works at an actual nuthouse!"

"It's not a nuthouse," I said. "It's an institution for the mentally handicapped."

"Same difference. Christ. It's like fucking a prison guard." She looked at me sideways with a kind of half-smile, half-smirk. I couldn't tell whether she was angry or joking.

"I'm a one-to-one counsellor," I said, pulling the covers up over my chest.

Shirley-Butch pulled the covers back down and ran her fingers lightly over one nipple, watching me. "I've never understood the appeal of prison guard fantasies," she mused.

"I'm not a prison guard!" I said.

She brushed my nipple again, casually. She had big, sure hands with bitten nails. "I guess it's just not my kink," she said. Her hand drifted down below the sheets, tangled in my pubic hair for a teasing second, and drifted back, tracing the scars up my arm. "Or maybe all those months I spent locked up in the loony bin just spoiled it for me."

She didn't look like she was intending to leap out of bed at that exact second, but it still wasn't the response I'd been looking for when I revealed my professional credentials.

41

THE CLOSET

"On the one hand, you went to that kiddy clinic when you were a teenager," Shirley-Butch shouted over the disco roar of Sappho's. "I can relate to that. And I must admit, your scars are more impressive than mine."

"Yours are not bad," I said kindly. She had a delicate silver latticework up her left arm, not like my thick ridges.

"But on the other hand," she continued, waving her other hand in the air in case I didn't get it, "being an outpatient is like being an inmate in the same way that doing paid housework for a few hours a week is like being a live-in domestic worker. And besides, you hide it. You're in the closet. How can I date a closet nutcase?"

"How can I date an obnoxious jerk like you, when I have a perfectly good girlfriend who never insults me?" I yelled back.

"You like me," she said, putting her tongue in my ear.

Or maybe it was David Bowie singing "Young Americans." Maybe Diane was twitching in her seat, wishing she was out on the dance floor throwing her body around to the angry words behind that beat. Maybe it was "Rebel, Rebel," that ode to tough femmes of every sex and gender. This was back when David Bowie was still a queen.

It was true.

BASEMENT

Stuart and I were wandering around touching things and I had to pee. What I should have done was walk back to Ward 5, park Stuart in a chair and use the Ward 5 staff washroom, but we were all the way across the grounds and Stuart was a really slow walker.

We went into the administration building and down to the basement staff washroom. At the washroom door I hesitated a second, and then I left Stuart standing in the hallway.

When I came out, he was gone.

"Damn, damn, damn," I muttered, checking down the hallway and up the stairs. No Stuart. I went back to the basement and tried each door. Most were locked, thank god, the ones with words like Furnace Room and Electrical printed on them. One door opened onto a small, dusty room with concrete walls and a square of indoor/outdoor carpet. Empty. The next room was the same. The next. Ripped the breath from my lungs. A half-naked tangle of bodies, frozen as I was frozen in startled terror. My breath came back. Not Stuart. Pat. Shirley's friend Pat from Ward D. And some guy. A skinny white guy with a lopsided face. I think he was from Ward 3. He stared at me, like a rabbit in the headlights the second before your car hits it. Pat held him tightly and looked off into the corner, as if something crucial was there in the shadows.

I turned around and walked out, closing the door behind me.

Stuart was outside on the lawn, standing in the sunlight, grinning and rocking.

And besides, I didn't want to go back to Ward 5 yet.

It just wouldn't look right to bring him in with me.

But I hurried. I really did. I didn't even look at Honeymoon for Nurse Holly.

43

HOW TO SIGN

I was sitting beside Mary on Ward D, with a chocolate bar in my pocket, doing the usual. Point to the red book. Point to the blue hat. We'd been doing it for months.

Or was it only days?

Mary seemed more bored than angry by this time, answering my commands with swift, contemptuous gestures.

"Will you teach me how to sign?" Geneva asked.

"I don't know how to sign," I said.

Geneva took that as shut-up-and-leave-me-alone and backed off. But it was true. I didn't know how to sign. This revelation came to me while reading the introduction to Dr. Carlson's big thick book on signing. American Sign Language (the book informed me) is a complex language with its own grammar and syntax, regional accents, slang. Learning sign from the skinny picture book was like learning English from a preschool alphabet book. A is for apple. B is for ball. On the other hand, learning sign from the big thick book would be like trying to learn English from a treatise on linguistics.

Besides, just getting through the introduction had taken me hours.

Probably there were night school classes where I could really learn to sign. And then after a year or so, I might be able to understand enough to start building on the signing Mary remembered from before Sunnybrook. And then I could bribe her with candy bars and the threat of my authority into having conversations with me. And maybe someday someone else on Ward D would learn sign too, and she could be forced to talk to them. It all seemed very jolly.

I added it to my long list of things I was going to learn at night school.

"Your shoelaces don't match," Geneva said. "One's black and one's brown."

"Thanks," I said.

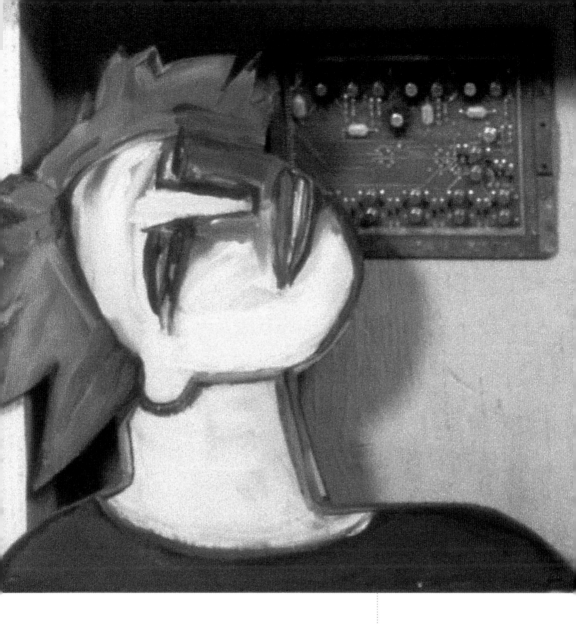

HOW TO TALK

Janey and I had an hour every morning and an hour
every afternoon which we used to get as far away from
Ward B as we could, and then come back.

We walked all the way to the gate, trailing sticks along
the bars of the perimeter fence for the sound of it. Then
we played volleyball with a piece of scrunched up paper

Or until I fell
down, which
invariably →
happened
first.

Sometimes I
thought I could
teach stuff to
Janey that would
actually be useful
to her. I thought
if she could learn
to say what she
wanted in words,
it might keep her
out of the side-
room. I thought it
was a pretty good
idea. I thought I
got it from this
assertiveness
training class
that my girlfriend
told me about, but
it actually wasn't
from there. It was
from before that.

*Diane learned that
one when she was
working as a cleaner
at a daycare centre.*

from the trash can behind Ward 3 and loud sound effects provided by Janey. Then we ran until we fell down.

Janey talked to me, the kind of talk that I was supposed to ignore because it was inappropriate and unresponsive. But that was OK, she didn't expect an answer, so I could tell myself I was ignoring her or listening to her, whichever I preferred.

"Shut up, Janey!" she said. "Be quiet!" She hit herself in the face and laughed. "You're in trouble now! Bad girl! Shut up!" She hit herself again. She seemed to find it funny. I tried it a few times. It hurt.

At the end of our time, we cut across the lawn back toward Ward B. That's what we did, every day. The hard part was walking past the administration building. There was something Janey didn't like about the administration building. As we came close to it, she tried to pull me in the other direction.

I went a little nearer and then asked her, "Do you want to go this way?"

She didn't say anything, but I could tell she really didn't like it. I waited a minute and asked her again. She started screaming quietly and pulling at my jacket. It was kind of scary. I'd heard so many bad stories about Janey.

"Tell me what you want," I said, avoiding her flailing arms. She grabbed me and started beating her head against my chest. I could feel the strength of her.

"Tell me! Use your words!"

"No," she said. "No."

"OK, right, good!"

I took off across the lawn, away from there. That's what we did, every day. Janey ran with me until I was out of breath. By then she was back to singing.

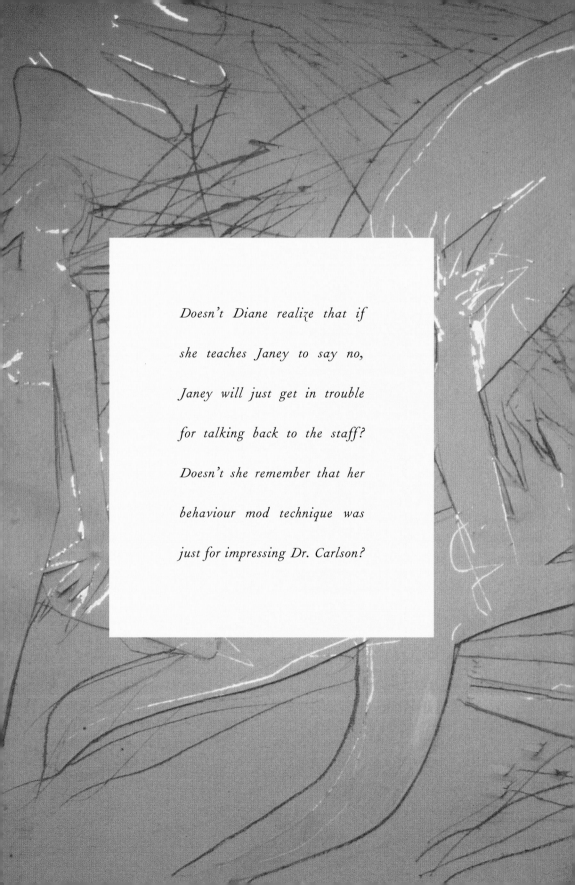

Doesn't Diane realize that if she teaches Janey to say no, Janey will just get in trouble for talking back to the staff? Doesn't she remember that her behaviour mod technique was just for impressing Dr. Carlson?

REAL

I was finished for the day, walking across the grounds and down to the main gate, like every day, the long walk down to the gate, clutching my keys. I had a key to the main gate. I could get out. I could leave whenever I wanted to. I wasn't an inmate.

Dr. Carlson told me I was doing a good job. At our last meeting he said the nursing staff was pleased with my work. He said he liked my reports. He acted like it was really true.

Maybe I was doing a good job. I considered that possibility as I walked down to the gate. Maybe they'd keep me on, even after the government took away their one-to-one counsellor money. It could be real, like a career, and not just one more in a long series of short jobs.

I could take night school classes. My girlfriend could help me type my papers, and I could learn how to write things with footnotes.

And look up things in the library. And read serious books. And memorize things for tests.

I know I said Diane stopped clutching her keys after the first few days, but that was another chapter. In this chapter, she's still clutching her keys.

You can do it. Come on. Everyone has trouble at first. Just try. Just try harder. You're not trying. You're lazy. You're selfish. You're irresponsible. Just try. Try harder. You're not trying.

Or maybe I wouldn't take a class. Maybe it would be OK if I just kept faking it. They seemed to like the way I was faking it, so far.

There was a security guard near the gate. What if he stopped me? What if he thought I was an inmate and wouldn't let me out? I could tell him I was a staff person. I could show him my keys. I could quote Shakespeare— out, out damned spot. See, I know Shakespeare, I'm on staff, I can prove it.

The guard nodded to me as I unlocked the gate.

"Goodnight," I said, with my best Nurse Holly smile, and made my escape.

Dr. Peters thought Holly was a frivolous light-weight because she joked around a lot. But Holly was actually very serious about nursing. Ever since she was a little girl, bandaging her dolls' cuts and bruises, she had longed to be a nurse. "I want to help people," she told her friends with a toss of her blonde curls. "If all I can do is make someone a little more comfortable in their hour of pain, then my life will have served some purpose."

LIGHT MY LIFE

Despite the fact that I'd never read a book about nurses before, everything in Holly's life seemed familiar. Her friends, her clothes, her dedication to her job, all had a rightness, an inevitability, like a truck bearing down on you while you stand frozen in the crosswalk.

My outfits had degenerated since my interview, but I was still trying, combing Value Village for professional pantsuits that didn't make me look like a kid on Halloween. I brushed my hair doggedly, trying to find a style with a bit more sophistication than a braid down the back. But every time I put it up, it fell back down within seconds, shedding bobby pins right and left.

"I work with retarded kids," I said to my face in the mirror, looking for a flicker of Florence Nightingale to light my life. But no amount of pinning could keep it in place.

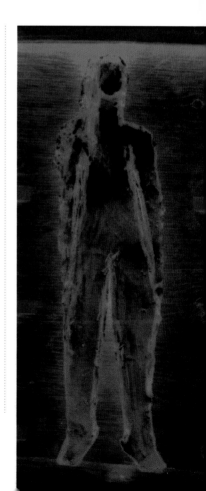

TELL

"You have to tell Nurse Thompson about Pat and that guy," my girlfriend said. We were eating take-out Chinese food at her kitchen table.

I choked on a water chestnut. "How can I tell Nurse Thompson? I'd get Pat in deep shit."

"Yeah, but Pat could be getting herself in deep shit, and you can't just stand by and act like you never saw anything. What if she gets pregnant?"

"I don't know. I didn't really think about that."

"Exactly. So think about it. You don't know if she's on contraceptives or sterilized or what. You don't even know what's wrong with her. What if it's something genetic? Do you want to see her have a child who ends up living its whole life at Sunnybrook?"

"I don't know," I said. The room seemed bright and distant, like a little doll house kitchen with table, chairs and tiny plates of food. I could hear the neighbours' TV: music, voices, gunshots.

"Why would she be sterilized?" I asked.

"I think they do that in cases where someone might be passing on faulty genes, or maybe it's if they couldn't take care of a baby. I'm not sure."

"I'd rather have Pat for a mother than Dr. Carlson," I said.

"That's not the point. The point is you don't have enough information to make a decision on your own. You've got to talk to someone. You can't just do nothing."

"If you were pregnant and you knew your child was going to grow up to be a shrink, would you get an abortion?" I asked.

"Come on, Persimmon. This is important."

"I can't tell on Pat," I said. I kept on repeating it until the conversation was over.

LIES

"So have you told the girlfriend?" Shirley-Butch asked. We were sitting in Sappho's, sweaty and breathless from "Personality Crisis" by the New York Dolls.

It didn't really seem like the right time to spring a question like that on me, but Shirley-Butch had no manners.

"Told her what?" I asked.

"Oh, I don't know. Told her you can't read. Told her you drink too much. Told her you're fucking some chick you picked up in the bar."

"I can read! I just read slowly, OK?"

"OK, OK. It was the last one I was really wondering about. The one about the chick."

I looked deeply into my beer mug, but found no answers.

"Not yet," I said.

"Why doesn't that surprise me?" Shirley-Butch asked.

"Why are you such an asshole?" I asked.

Shirley-Butch laughed and pulled me off my chair and onto her lap.

"You tell so many lies it's a wonder you can keep track of who you are."

I considered getting angry and starting a fight, but I was far too comfortable on Shirley-Butch's lap.

She had both arms around me, and her mouth was working its way up my neck, alternating kisses and soft little bites. When she got to my ear, she whispered, "Want to dance?"

"Sure," I whispered back.

"OK, but let's wait for a slow one. When the next slow one comes on, I'm going to take you out onto the dance floor, and I'm going to dance very close to you. OK?"

"Sure," I said.

"There'll be just an inch or two between us," Shirley-

It's my disco and I'll lie if I want to.

I was off tequila, being currently more interested in mild intoxication than complete oblivion.

It didn't seem like lying. It was more like a whole other world that didn't involve my girlfriend. It was like my girlfriend was in this one world where I was a budding young social service professional who might go back to school, and Shirley-Butch was in this other world where I had graduated from the child guidance centre with a major in fucking up.

Butch whispered. "I'll be so close that your nipples will feel the heat from my sweat, but I'll keep those few inches between us. When you move closer, I'll back off just a bit. Just enough. This might only go on for a few minutes, but it'll seem like a long time to you because your cunt will be starting to ache."

I could feel my heart beating in my clit, right on cue, like some girl-group dancing in perfect synch to Shirley-Butch's lead.

"I'll be watching you," she said, "as you ache more and more. Then I'll let you brush up against me every now and then, just for a second. A burning second. Then I'll pull away. When I can see that you're having trouble breathing then I'll grab you. It'll probably be a fast song by then, but I'll keep dancing very slow. You'll be giving me those let's-go-back-to-your-place signals and wondering why I'm not picking up on them. Your legs will be shaking. Your jeans will be damp. I'll shove my leg between yours and you'll start to move on me. You won't be able to help yourself. You'll be making a scene on the dance floor, but what the hell. The bartender likes you, she's not going to complain. Finally you'll whisper in my ear, 'Take me home with you.' 'Huh?' I'll say. 'Please take me home,' you'll say. 'But I like this song,' I'll say. 'I like it a lot.' Maybe I'll like the next song too, and the one after that. Or maybe I'll take pity on you and bring you back to my place and fuck you till you scream for me.

It was like when I was in grade six and the principal sent me to the shrink's office for the crime of hating school. I had to go once a week during recess. I was supposed to wait until everyone else had gone outside and then sneak through this unmarked door next to the nurse's office. If anyone asked I was supposed to tell them I hadn't been feeling well and was going to the nurse's to lie down. If the school tells you to say it, how can

And the next time you see your girlfriend you can tell her any goddamn thing you like."

"OK," I said.

it be a lie? The only kids it was safe to talk to were the other ones who dawdled on their way to recess once a week. When you knew what to look for, they were easy to spot.

It was like when I was in high school and I used to take out books with important titles and display them casually on my desk. "Oh yeah, it's a real cool book. You should read it." I wasn't lying. I was just trying to live in the same world as the other kids. The ones who never missed recess.

HOW TO WRITE

It didn't seem like the kind of thing you should say to your boss.

I had a meeting about Mary with Dr. Carlson. I didn't tell him that I couldn't learn to sign from his books.

Instead, I suggested that I try to teach Mary how to write. It seemed like a good idea to me. It would be a more practical way for her to communicate than signing, since most of the staff could probably read. Plus it was something I actually knew how to do, so I wouldn't be faking it.

"I think she could do it," I told him. "She's very fast."

I COULD read. I was just kind of slow. OK, very slow.

Dr. Carlson looked at me, amusement and irritation warring on his face. He let amusement win. "I'm afraid you're being rather unrealistic," he said with a forgiving chuckle. "Go back and re-read her file. You'll see that she has been thoroughly tested, as are all our residents. She falls within the range of Trainably Mentally Handicapped, but far below Teachably Mentally Handicapped, which is the category she'd have to be in to learn to read and write. The fact that she remembers some rudimentary signing from her childhood is very good. But don't let it blind you to her very significant deficits. You aren't doing her any favours by placing expectations on her that are so far above her capabilities. Now, was there anything else?"

"No," I said, "that's all."

I wondered what kind of tests Mary had taken. I tried to imagine her struggling to do her best on a series of arcane exercises that would reveal everything and set her level forever. I could see a nice lady with a warm smile and curly blonde hair administering the tests. First she was smiling and then she was cradling her broken fingers. No matter how hard I tried, I couldn't make the scene go any differently.

I guess my imagination just wasn't that good.

54

SHOES

The head nurse on Ward 5 was so pleased with my work that she asked me to teach Stuart to tie his shoes. "You can do it every day, after his shave," she said.

"OK," I said.

Cheerful and
obedient.
The good employee.

I could remember learning to tie my

shoes. I could remember my sweating hands,

fingers swollen with clumsiness. Knots that

refused to bow / tiny knots tearing my

fingernails / pulling tighter till my shoes

I'm a nice girl.
I'm whatever you
expect to see.
I come from a
family just like
yours. A nice
family.

were knotted shut. I remember jerking at

the laces, knowing I was just making it

worse / making it worse. I can remember

the itching heat inside my skin / I can't /

can't / banging my head on the wall to

hurt myself / hurt myself.

But of course it wasn't like that.

Of course.

Stuart laughed and tasted the laces and tried to follow my directions. He didn't get upset. He didn't care if he could tie his shoes or not. But if I wanted to play with his shoes, he'd go along with it.

I wasn't sure if I was breaking some behaviour mod rule. I thought I probably was, but you never knew how these things worked from ward to ward and I wasn't going to ask. That way if I got caught I could plead ignorance.

As usual.

SIDEROOM

The next morning Janey was in the sideroom, so I spent an hour in the basement staff washroom with Nurse Holly. When I looked in the afternoon, Janey was there again (or maybe still). This time, after checking the hallway for staff, I unlocked the door and slipped in.

She was sitting on the floor in her favourite corner, singing quietly. When I took a step toward her, she started screaming and biting her arms which were already kind of bloody.

"OK, sure, I'll stay back here," I told her. It didn't seem like the time to push her on using words, and anyway, her meaning was perfectly clear.

I sat down with my back to the door, which gave me the double advantage of being out of sight from any passing nurse and out of Janey's current sphere of discomfort. Janey and I sat there looking at each other. Five or ten minutes passed.

"Well, here we are," I said.

Janey looked at me.

"So what do you do for fun around this joint?" I asked.

Janey looked at me.

"If we can sneak past Nurse Jones we could go outside."

"Outside," Janey said.

I reached my hand toward her and she started screaming. I pulled it back.

"OK, not yet. Fine. So. Do you know any songs besides 'The Sound of Music'?"

Janey looked at me.

"How about 'Free Money' by Patti Smith? I bet they never played that for you in here."

She looked at me. I sang the first line. She looked at me. I sang it again, and she sang with me in a tuneless, wordless kind of way. The second time she was better. By the end of the hour she had it down: "Oh baby," we sang, "It would mean so much to me." ←————— To buy you all the things you need for free.

FAVOURITE THINGS

I stopped short
of teaching her
"Gloria." I
didn't want her
to get in even
more trouble.

The next day Janey was in the sideroom again, and the next day and the next. Sometimes she was wearing a strait jacket and sometimes she was just in there. By the end of the week Janey had learned "Free Money," "Redondo Beach" and most of "Break It Up." I had learned "The Lonely Goatherd" and "These Are a Few of My Favourite Things."

I stopped by Nurse Jones' office on Friday.

"Can I look at the staff log?" I asked.

"Sure, help yourself."

I read the week's entry over three times, but all it said about Janey was, "Difficult. Much time in sideroom," which I already knew. I put the log away and turned to Nurse Jones. "Do you know what's been going on with Janey?" I asked.

"You mean besides throwing her dinner on the floor and attacking an orderly?"

"Well do you have any idea why it's happening?"

"Oh, she's just acting out."

Thank you.
That explains
everything.

My feet wanted to leave. My stomach was telling me it was a stupid waste of time. But I persevered. "Isn't it a bit strange for her to do it all week?"

"What can I say? It's been a week of acting out. She'll settle down eventually."

"Yes but if there was a reason we could figure out . . ."

Nurse Jones shook her head, looking up at me with a smile that was a thousand years old and sick of it. "I've

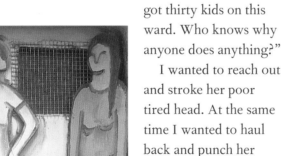

got thirty kids on this ward. Who knows why anyone does anything?"

I wanted to reach out and stroke her poor tired head. At the same time I wanted to haul back and punch her face in.

"OK," I said. "Well. See ya." I walked out of her office, down the hall and through the Ward B door.

"Thank God it's Friday," I muttered under my breath. ←

Have a nice weekend, Janey.

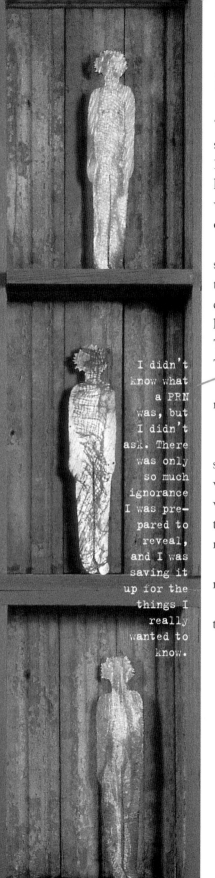

I didn't
know what
a PRN
was, but
I didn't
ask. There
was only
so much
ignorance
I was pre-
pared to
reveal,
and I was
saving it
up for the
things I
really
wanted to
know.

STRAIT

"What I don't understand is why they put someone in a strait jacket *and* in solitary confinement at the same time. Isn't that kind of overkill?" I asked Shirley-Butch. I was lying in her narrow bed, my clothes all undone, soaked with her sweat and mine. Shirley-Butch was leaning on one elbow, absent-mindedly playing with my ears.

"I think it's related to nuclear deterrent theory," she said. "Why control someone once if you can control them two or three times over. Probably Janey's pumped full of chemical strait jacket too. Haldol, chlorpromazine, I don't know what. Maybe some new modern miracle thing. They always have a new modern miracle thing going. Then there'd probably be a PRN on top of that."

I held Shirley-Butch silently for awhile, breathing our rich, rank smell, rehearsing my next inquiry.

"Were you ever in a strait jacket?"

I could feel the flinch in her body. Bad question. But she laughed and cuffed the side of my head lightly. "Who wants to know? What's it to you?" She grazed my jaw with a soft fist and then stuck her fingers in my mouth as I tried to answer. I bit down just hard enough to make her remove her hand in a hurry.

"I just wondered, OK?" I managed to say before she rolled us both off the bed, landing squarely on top of me.

"What am I going to do with you?" she asked, and then proceeded to show me.

THE WIND

"I've never even seen a strait jacket," Shirley-Butch said afterwards, lying on the floor in a tangle of blankets. "Strait jackets seem so . . . old fashioned. Where I was, they used four point restraints; they put you on this table thing and tied your arms and legs to it. Very uncomfortable." She sighed and shook her head. "Jesus. I was so young then. My first real job after high school. Working in a box factory, making boxes. And God was talking to me. It was amazing. It was like this big wind blowing through me, telling me things. I know a lot of people have a really bad time when they're crazy, but I liked it. I liked that wind. But my parents were scared shitless and they brought me in. They said we were just going for a drive, and then all of a sudden we were at the loony bin and these two big guys were dragging me inside. I tried to fight, but they shot me up and took my clothes off and tied me onto the table and left me alone in a locked cell. Talk about overkill. It was cold."

She punched me again, softly but not quite playfully. "So. That's the story."

She looked at me for a long, silent moment and then rolled away, lying on her back, staring at the ceiling. ←

I kissed her cheekbones, smoothed out her ruffled hair and then mussed it up again. She pushed my hands away.

"OK, your turn," she said, suddenly turning her hot eyes on me. "Are you going to talk to me or are you just going to lie and smile like you do in the rest of your life?"

"OK," I said. "OK. I hate flipping out and God never talks to me. Who wants to know?"

It was a very plain ceiling, white with no cracks, but she watched it for a long time.

Maybe I said other things. Maybe I gave every scar a name that night. But I'm not going to name them for you.

PAT

I was walking down the sidewalk toward Ward D when I saw Pat coming out the door. I'd been looking for a chance to talk to her alone all week with no luck, so I ran to catch up to her.

"Hi Pat," I said.

"I'm going to OT," she said.

"Great. I'll walk you over there."

But Pat seemed to have developed a sudden fascination with her shoes. She stood there, staring at them.

"Umm, actually, I really wanted to talk to you," I said.

Pat was rotating her right foot like you would if you were putting out a cigarette butt on the sidewalk, making very sure there wasn't a single spark left that might start a forest fire.

"I was just, you know, wondering what's happening with you and that guy from Ward 3."

Pat shook her head without meeting my eyes. If there had been a cigarette butt, it would have been dust by now.

"I mean, if there's anything I can do to help . . ."

"I have to go to OT," Pat said. Her eyes darted past me, looking for rescue across the empty lawn.

"It's OK," I said.

For a brief second she looked up.

It wasn't fear.
It was anger.

Then she looked away. The atoms of the cigarette butt were bonded to the atoms of the sidewalk.

"I'm sorry," I said. "Go to OT." And she did.

GOOD KIDS

Stuart and I had been doing our shoe routine for a few days when one of the Ward 5 orderlies sat down beside me.

"This is none of my business," he said, "but you could just shave Stuart and tie his shoes for him and take him off the ward. He never gets off the ward."

"I know," I said, "but Nurse Lau wants him to learn to do stuff himself. So he can . . . you know . . . be more independent."

She was still playing the good employee. Or the good employee was playing her.

"Dream on," the orderly said.

"What do you mean? Stuart can learn things. He can learn lots of things!"

The orderly laughed. "Not in this place. You know what he does all day? He sits. All day. No one even talks to him. We're too busy. Good kids get ignored, bad kids get punished— that's how it works. An hour a day with you isn't going to change anything. And he likes to go outside."

I looked at Stuart. He was rocking back and forth, waiting for something to happen, or nothing. I looked at the orderly.

I didn't know how to talk to this guy. I sounded like Nurse Holly. It was frightening.

"I'm supposed to be teaching him something, not just tying his shoes."

"Oh right. You're too important to tie someone's shoes. That's the orderlies' job. You're psych staff. You're above that."

"That's bullshit!" I said.

I felt better. Nurse Holly would never talk like that.

"Oh yeah? Is it? I bet you don't even know the names of any of the orderlies."

"Your name's Diane," he said. "You've worked here for three months and your supervisor is Dr. Carlson. Right?"

He stood up. I thought he was going to walk off, but he held out his hand. "Hi," he said. "My name's Michel."

I tried to think of an answer, but there was no answer.

HELP

"Why would Pat talk to you?" Shirley-Butch asked. We were sitting in her basement apartment, having morning-after coffee, and I was asking her what I should do about Pat.

"She needs to talk to someone," I answered.

Shirley-Butch sipped her coffee and considered that. "Maybe, maybe not. But if I was Pat, I'd talk to one of the other Ward D girls. Or to the boyfriend. She obviously has a whole life that you know nothing about. Staff always think they're the most important thing in the inmates' lives, but believe me, you're not."

"I have a good relationship with Pat," I said.

"But why would she talk to staff about things that could get her in trouble?"

"I know. I need to somehow convince her that I don't want to get her in trouble. I want to help."

Shirley-Butch got up and walked over to the window. It was about two steps away. Her apartment was very small. She stood there, looking out into the back garden for a few seconds, and then she came back and sat down again. "Why would Pat want your help?" she said.

I could tell she was mad, but I wasn't sure what I had said wrong. Not knowing, it was hard to figure out how to say something else that would make her not mad. "I don't know. I mean . . . of course she should talk to her boyfriend too. Or whatever he is." There was no visible thaw, but I stumbled on. "Well, but, the thing is, maybe I could help her in ways that another inmate couldn't."

Shirley-Butch put her cup down. Actually she kind of slammed it down, sloshing coffee on the table. "Sure, Nancy Nurse. Just what do you think you can do for her? I know, first you can explain to Dr. Carlson that she's not really a kid. Then you can convince him to set up little cottages for married inmates. And then of course you'd

There was some-
thing about
Shirley-Butch
that made me ask
her things. I had
the same reaction
to Sunnybrook-
Shirley. It was
like I thought
they could explain
my whole life to
me if only they
would. But mostly
they wouldn't.

have to get it extended to common-law couples, and let's not forget same-sex relationships. And there could be a motel for inmates who had something more casual in mind. And you'd have to design a series of sex education classes, ones that would make sense to Janey and Stuart as well as Pat and Mary. And you'd better have a class on rape prevention in there too, if it's anything like when I was locked up. If it wasn't some guy on the ward who wouldn't take no for an answer, it was some power-drunk staffer, doing it because he could get away with it."

"You make it all sound impossible," I said.

"It's possible, OK? But not in Sunnybrook."

"Yeah, but I can't just do nothing!" ←

"Why not? You've been doing nothing about a lot of fucked-up things in that place. Why change now, just because Pat has managed to make herself a bit of life that you're not in control of?"

"That's not fair!"

"No, it's not, but you know what? I don't give a shit."

I didn't know what to say to that, so I didn't say anything. Shirley-Butch got up and went into the bedroom. It was about three steps away, but there was a door and she closed it. After awhile I left.

That's what my girlfriend had said to me when I refused to tell Nurse Thompson. And now I was saying it to Shirley-Butch. Did I believe it? Did I think I should believe it? Was it what Florence Nightingale would have said?

I was trying to talk without moving my lips, like they do in prison movies, because an orderly was coming down the hall toward us.

ACTUALLY TALK

Shirley was sitting in the behaviour mod chair on Ward D.

"Hey nurse, guess what?" she said.

"I'm not a nurse," I said.

"Nurse Thompson wants to see you in her office," the orderly said.

"Who me?" I said.

"Who do you think? I've already been there," Shirley said. "It's your turn now." But she took pity on me when I was halfway down the hall and yelled, "Don't worry, you're not in trouble. Mary is."

Nurse Thompson beamed at me when I walked into her office.

"I have something very exciting to tell you," she said. "We've discovered that Mary has some residual hearing. She seems to be able to hear very loud noises. We think it's enough to make a hearing aid practical. We'll have to get her tested. Then Dr. Carlson is going to get you some books on speech therapy. If she can hear, you can teach her to actually talk."

"Wow," I said. "This is really . . . I mean . . . what a surprise."

"Yes, we're so pleased. And it was the other kids who discovered it. You know how Pat's been going on about 'Mary can hear, Mary can hear' for months now. And we all assumed it was just another of her attention-getting mechanisms.

"But then some of the other kids got together and insisted it was true. While we were watching, one of them snuck up behind Mary and yelled. And Mary turned around. They did it three times, and each time she responded. Well, that convinced us. We were so proud of those kids. They came up with the whole thing by them-selves. We might even call the local paper. I think it would make a great human interest story."

"Yeah," I said. "Really. Wow."

Twenty-nine years. Mary has lived here twenty-nine years.

SUGAR

I was too proud to
let it ring more
than ten times.

Everything's going
to be all right.
Everything's going
to be all right.

Shirley-Butch wasn't answering her phone. She wasn't at Sappho's either. The DJ was playing "Shame, Shame, Shame," urging my feet to jump, but I drank instead: beautiful tequila like frozen electricity in my mouth. One, two, three, many, until my mind slipped its leash and "Sugar Sugar" transformed itself into Bob Marley singing "No Woman No Cry."

In your dreams.

THE ACQUISITION
OF LANGUAGE

The books Dr. Carlson got for me to use with Mary were all densely written theoretical texts on the acquisition of language. I forced myself through a few pages, but it was useless. I couldn't read them.

Despite that, I was almost looking forward to Mary's first day with a hearing aid. But when I came onto Ward D that morning, another orderly told me to report to the office.

Nurse Thompson was leaning against her desk, staring out the window. She straightened up when I came in.

"Bad news," she said. "Mary broke her hearing aid. We put it on her last night after dinner and it was OK for a few hours. But then she just took it out and stepped on it."

Nurse Thompson sighed. "She doesn't understand. But how many hearing aids can we let her break? They're just too expensive. I don't know if Requisitions will approve another one, unless we can guarantee she'll use it. And we can't. You know Mary. She'll do it again."

"Yeah," I said. "I know. But it's worth a try, right?"

Nurse Thompson sighed. I sighed. I didn't know why I hadn't seen it coming. Mary was always so thoroughly and stubbornly Mary.

I wondered if I'd do the same in her place.

You couldn't. You'd give in. You'd give in.

I knew I could get my girlfriend to explain them to me. She was always reading serious stuff and telling me about it. But I couldn't ask her. Somehow it wasn't the same as getting her to type a report.

I'd never seen her look so miserable.

SIDE OF THE FENCE

I was finished for the day, walking across the grounds and down to the main gate, like I did every day.

I said good night to the security guard and walked out into the bright summer evening. Shirley-Butch was parked down the road in an old beat-up Rambler.

She had the motor running and the window rolled down. She looked cute and unpredictable. I walked over and leaned against the side of the car.

"Hi there, stranger," I said, in my best Mae West voice.

"Hi Diane."

She looked me up and down and smiled, taking in my briefcase, my nearly professional pantsuit. I straightened up. I could tell she wasn't here for a big reconciliation scene.

"Don't call me that, OK? My name's Persimmon."

"Oh right. It's so hard to keep up with your many identities." She was leaning back, relaxed and casual, like she was enjoying our little chat. But her eyes were hard.

"If you want to fight, let's go somewhere else," I said.

"I thought you could give me a tour of Sunnybrook," she said.

"It's late."

"It's only quarter to five. Come on."

"Let's just go somewhere," I said.

"Yeah, let's go visit Janey on Ward B."

If I had ever put any thought into what kind of car Shirley-Butch would drive, an old beat-up Rambler is what I would have guessed.

70

"No." I stepped back and gave her a serious cut-the-crap glare which she ignored.

"But she's like your best friend. I want to meet her."

"I just want to go home, OK?"

"I want to see where you work. Come on, introduce me to your other life. Don't worry, I've been in places like this before. I know how to act."

"Please. I don't want to fight with you."

"I'd feel right at home. Mary and I could bond over behaviour mod techniques we have known." Shirley-Butch revved her engine and I jumped back.

"Stop it," I said.

She paid no attention. She was on a roll. "And maybe you could finally decide which side of the fence you're on," she said.

"Why does there have to be a fence?"

"There doesn't have to be a fence. But there is a fence. It's right behind you and there's a guard at the gate."

I stood there, my briefcase in one hand. A Value Village special. I couldn't think of a single snappy comeback.

"Make up your mind, honey," she said, and pulled away with an impressive squeal of tires. I watched the Rambler disappear down the road, and then started the long trek up the hill toward the bus stop.

I sounded like Nurse Holly being sweet and ineffectual in the face of some convoluted misunderstanding with Dr. Peters. But I knew there was no misunderstanding.

I sounded like some New Age self-help book, except this was before New Age.

By now Nurse Holly was desperately in love with Dr. Peters. She longed to be crushed in his steely embrace. But she was sure he didn't like her, so she treated him with icy politeness, which made him think she didn't like him, so he treated her with icy politeness too. This went on and on.

LONGED
FOR

A week passed. Two weeks. I seemed to be spending more and more time in the administration building basement staff washroom. I would read or cry or just sit there trying not to think about my job.

I wondered who had left *Honeymoon for Nurse Holly* on the back of the toilet. Was it a nurse who longed for a steely embrace to distract her from the smell of piss and Lysol?

None of the nurses I knew seemed like the type. They weren't that naive. If they longed for anything, it was the end of their shift.

One of the good things about being a slow reader is that one book lasts a long time.

ON THE GRASS

This man had to decide whether to risk all his winnings for a chance at another $10,000, or just quit and keep what he had. It was a tense moment.

Stuart was sitting on the same chair, in the same corner. He was rocking. All around him other people were rocking. The TV was tuned to a game show.

Michel waved at me from across the ward. He was watching me. Nurse Lau was watching me. Shirley-Butch was watching me. My girlfriend was watching me. Everyone in my life was watching me except for Stuart and his Ward 5 pals. They were watching the game show music.

"Hi Stuart," I said. He turned toward my voice.

"Diane," he said, smelling my hand, grinning his sweet Frankenstein smile.

"See? Stuart likes me," I said to Shirley-Butch. But she wasn't impressed. She was somewhere else, mad at me.

I wanted to be somewhere else, another country maybe, or a small dark room where no one could see that I didn't know how to do things the way they're supposed to be done, the way the kids who don't miss recess are born knowing, the way I have never been able to figure out.

"Let's practice shaving," I said out loud, putting the electric razor in Stuart's hands. He shaved, grinning, laughing, patting my arm with his free hand. I could hear the wordless moans of the other inmates under the excited voice of the game show host. Someone had just won something. My skin was screaming.

"Let's go outside," I said, grabbing the razor, even though Stuart was only halfway done and we hadn't practiced his shoe-tying. Stuart took my hand, stood slowly, walked slowly. I dumped the razor on Nurse Lau's desk and pulled Stuart through the Ward 5 door.

Without cleaning it, bad girl.

Outside the air smelled like hot summer. We walked around touching things: the skinny little cedar tree, the

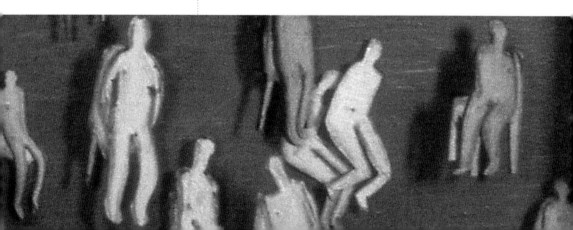

smooth-barked birch, the plastic siding on the OT building. We kicked trash barrels for the hollow thunk and slapped the metal lampposts to make them ring. I didn't ask him for words and he didn't give me any. He wasn't really interested in words.

"OK, let's try this," I said. "Let's sit down on the grass." I don't think Stuart understood what I meant. I sat down, pulling on his hand so he came with me. We had never sat on the grass before, only on benches.

He crouched there for a minute, stroking the manicured lawn, and then he lay face down, embracing it with his whole body, breathing the smell of grass and earth. I sat there, watching. I tried to weigh this moment against the hours of Ward 5 rocking, against Mary forced to play at signing and Janey in the sideroom. But I couldn't make it count. It was meaningless, crushed under the weight of institutional indifference.

"This is stupid," I told Stuart. "In half an hour you'll go back on the ward and nothing will have changed. So what's the point? There is no point."

Stuart turned toward the sound of my voice. His nose was smudged with dirt and little bits of grass were stuck to his face.

"Bushes," he said.

Apparently he disagreed.

I'd never seen anyone at Sunnybrook sitting on the grass

BUSY

Shirley and Pat and the skinny white guy from Ward 3 were sitting on the stone bench across the lawn from Ward D. As I came closer, the Ward 3 guy got up and walked off in the other direction.

I said hi as I passed Shirley and Pat, but I didn't stop. They were busy.

I hated how he flinched every time he saw me.

FLANNEL SHIRT

I was over at my girlfriend's house, watching "Star Trek." My girlfriend was in and out, sitting beside me for a few restless minutes and then leaping up to fuss with things in the kitchen. She never watched anything but the news and serious PBS documentaries.

McCoy had just been carried off by a large thing with tentacles and the scene had switched to a soup commercial when my girlfriend sat back down and muted the volume. She put her arms around me and looked into my eyes with her serious talk look.

"I know you're having a hard time," she said. "I wish I could do something."

"Yeah," I said. I snuggled deeper into her embrace. She had on a worn old flannel shirt that I loved. It smelled warm and clean like fresh dryer lint.

"Can I do something?" she asked. Her voice was soft with concern. I wished I could hide in the circle of her arms forever, but I knew I would come out again, if only to see what happened to McCoy.

"I don't know," I said. "It's just my stupid job. Or something."

She couldn't help me any more than I could help Pat or Janey. We were in different worlds. Love is supposed to break down those barriers.

We sat there in the dark for a long time, saying nothing, as Spock and Kirk battled large things with tentacles.

I had an ongoing interest in the jealous love-triangle of Spock, Kirk and McCoy.

Or at least that's what she told me. I suppose she could have had a secret "Partridge Family" addiction that I knew nothing about.

That's a lie. This was before remote control TV.

But if love just pretends those barriers don't exist, it's never going to break down anything.

CLOSED
BEHIND ME

Janey and I were coming through the
front doors onto Ward B. I was putting
my keys back on my belt when the door
at the other end of the hallway
slammed open.

I heard screaming.

Oh fuck, this is
going to upset
Janey.

I saw Shirley running down the hall toward us.
There was blood all over her face. Two orderlies were
chasing her.

She was screaming.

And then Janey was screaming. Janey was going to flip
out and get into trouble.

Goddamn you,
Shirley. Why do
you always have to
make such a big
production out of
everything?

Janey started hitting the wall with her fist, moving
down the hall a few steps, then a few more, sucked into
the current of violence like a leaf in a river. I grabbed
hold of her, but she shook me off.

Be quiet, Shirley.
Just this once,
keep it to
yourself.

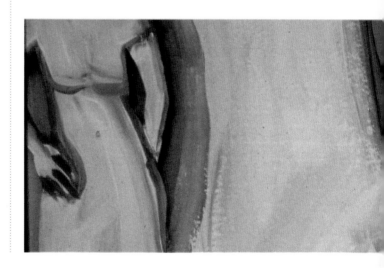

One of the orderlies tackled Shirley and they went down in a heap. There was a startled silence, an intake of breath. I heard what I had been thinking.

Shirley was lying on the floor with her hands over her bloody face. The first orderly was sitting on her.

This is Shirley. The real person Shirley.

The other orderly was running down the hall, toward Janey. "Help me!" he yelled to me. "I can't handle this one."

How could I look at you and see a nuisance thing, getting in the way, making my job harder? We're almost friends.

Janey was moving toward him, screaming, pounding the walls.

"Help me!" the orderly yelled. "This one's violent."
I turned around and walked out, unlocking the door with my Ward B key and letting it close behind me.

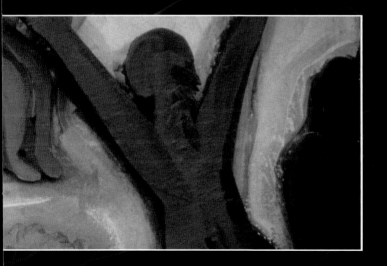

But we're not friends.

I'm on staff.

GO NOW

The next time I saw Shirley, she was sitting in the
dayroom on Ward B, wearing her green robe and fuzzy
slippers. There was a bandage taped to her forehead.

"Janey's in the sideroom," she said. "OK," I said. But
I just stood there. The dayroom echoed with noise and
need, a normal day.

"I hate this place," I said.

Shirley just looked at me.

"Do you really think I'm a nurse?" I asked.

"Your name is Diane," she said.

"Right," I said. "Right." I forced my feet to walk
across the dayroom.

"Hey nurse!" Shirley yelled. I turned around.

"You'd better go now," she said.

I thought she was probably right.

I knew in the
sideroom it would
be quieter, just
Janey singing or
screaming. I
couldn't move.
I was tired.

Another noise.

SEE THEM

I still see them on the street sometimes.

But it's
never them.

That was the ending for a long time, but now there's a different ending.

SHIRLEY

I walked out of Sunnybrook that day and never came back. I never even went to visit Janey. I've always felt guilty about that. "People live there twenty-four hours a day. What makes you so special and sensitive that you can't even make it through an hour every now and then?" I asked myself. My Self had no answer except the inarticulate refusal to pass through those gates.

I got used to seeing them around town, my heart turning over as Stuart walked down the sidewalk toward me and flashed me his goofy grin before turning into a stranger. Or Janey on the street corner joking around with a gang of girls, or Pat and her boyfriend necking in the back of the Number 25 bus, or Mary behind the till at the local supermarket, scowling at the customers.

I took this haunting as my due punishment for having left them. Then I saw Shirley at a workshop on Women and Disability.

She was part of a panel on lobbying the government. There were two other women on the panel, one who looked like she had cerebral palsy, and one who I couldn't tell what her disability was. I kept watching for Shirley's face to shift into someone else's, but she stayed Shirley. She was talking about the closure of Sunnybrook. She had the same slow, thick voice that you had to wait for and pay attention to, but the people in the audience seemed to be listening. Probably a lot of them were just being polite and were actually squirming inside from the effort of holding still for that voice, but what the hell. They could sit there and squirm and maybe eventually get used to it.

"The government just wanted to save money," Shirley said. "That's all. That's why they listened to us."

"Yeah, like where's the community support?" said the invisibly disabled one.

But it wasn't them. Of course it wasn't them.

This was years later. A lot had changed. I was tough enough to go to a Women and Disability workshop. I could even say the words Learning Disabled out loud without choking on them.

That's a lie. Diane tried to write the sentence about not choking three different times and each time there was another good reason not to say the words Learning Disabled. One: the sentence before is clear enough, you don't need further explanations. Two: focussing on how much Diane has changed is too "happy ending."

Three: Learning Disabled is really just another psychiatric label used to divide people into normal and not normal, and you shouldn't use it without explaining how labels like that are arbitrary and oppressive, but can sometimes be useful to those of us who would be invisible otherwise —which would be much too complicated and rhetorical to get into at this point. In the end, Diane only wrote the words Learning Disabled under intense pressure from her writing group. So obviously she's still choking.

"Yeah, if you think shutting down Sunnybrook means everyone's all fine, well excuse me, there's some boarding homes I'd like you to see," said the CP-looking one.

"Yeah," said Shirley, "excuse me. They take your welfare cheque and give you like two dollars a day."

I wasn't used to Shirley making speeches. I mean, she had a reputation on Ward D as a big talker, but her sentences were always chopped up with sidelong glances to see if she was in trouble yet. I wondered how long it had taken her to learn to stop checking. I wondered about a lot of things, but I wasn't sure what was OK to ask.

When I went up to her afterwards, I could tell she didn't recognize me.

"I knew you years ago, on Ward D," I said.

"Oh yeah?"

"I worked with Mary."

"Oh yeah, I remember you." She grinned at me, but her eyes were wary.

"When did you get out?" I asked. It was a neutral question, not like where did they put Janey, or are you really a lesbian.

"A few years ago. Everyone's out now."

"So what are you doing these days?"

"Different stuff. The newsletter sometimes, *The Self Advocate*. You can buy one from Doreen. She works on it a lot. I mostly go to the park and pick up litter."

"Is that like a city job?"

"Oh yeah, city job. Don't hold your breath. I just do it. For the environment. Some days I get three big garbage bags full." She looked over her shoulder to where the other women from the panel were waiting for her. I decided to risk one more question.

"How come you set that fire on Ward D?"

Shirley smirked. "Oh right. My fires. Right. I made a fire every year for four years. To burn down Ward D. Then the closure thing started and I got into that instead."

"So it was like a protest?"

"It was because I hated it."

"That's what I thought! Or maybe you told me. But Nurse Thompson said it was just Fire-Starting Behaviour." ←

I didn't realize until that moment that part of me had actually believed Nurse Thompson over Shirley and my own common sense for all these years. She was, after all, a professional, and what was I? A fucked-up kid.

"Yeah, right. Nurse Thompson." Shirley rolled her eyes. "There was a lot going on that you guys didn't know about."

A woman with shaky hands and a motorized chair rolled up to Shirley and poked her in the ribs. "Let's go, kiddo."

"OK," Shirley said, "see you later," and headed for the door.

"Bye," I said.

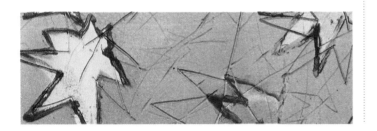

Persimmon Blackbridge is an internationally acclaimed writer and visual artist. As a member of the Kiss & Tell collective, she is co-author of the 1995 Lambda Literary Award-winning *Her Tongue on My Theory* and the postcard book *Drawing the Line*. Blackbridge is also co-author, with Sheila Gilhooly, of the "mad movement" classic *Still Sane*. *Sunnybrook* is her first novel.

Winner of the prestigious VIVA visual arts award, Blackbridge has exhibited widely across Canada and the United Sates, as well as in Australia, Europe and Hong Kong. A learning-disabled-lesbian-cleaning-lady-sculptor-performer-video-artist, she is currently working on her next book, which is about sex, madness and the Internet.

Press Gang Publishers has been producing vital and provocative books by women since 1975.

A free catalogue is available from Press Gang Publishers, #101 - 225 East 17th Avenue, Vancouver, B.C. V5V 1A6 Canada